Peppa Pig™

The Train Ride

Today Madame Gazelle, Peppa and her friends are going on a train ride.

"Can I see your tickets, please?"
Mr Rabbit asks them.
The children wave their tickets in the air.
"Oh no! I've lost my ticket!" Pedro cries.
"There's your ticket!" Madame Gazelle
says, pointing to a ticket on the ground.

"Try not to lose it again," says Mr Rabbit, smiling at Pedro.

Phwee!

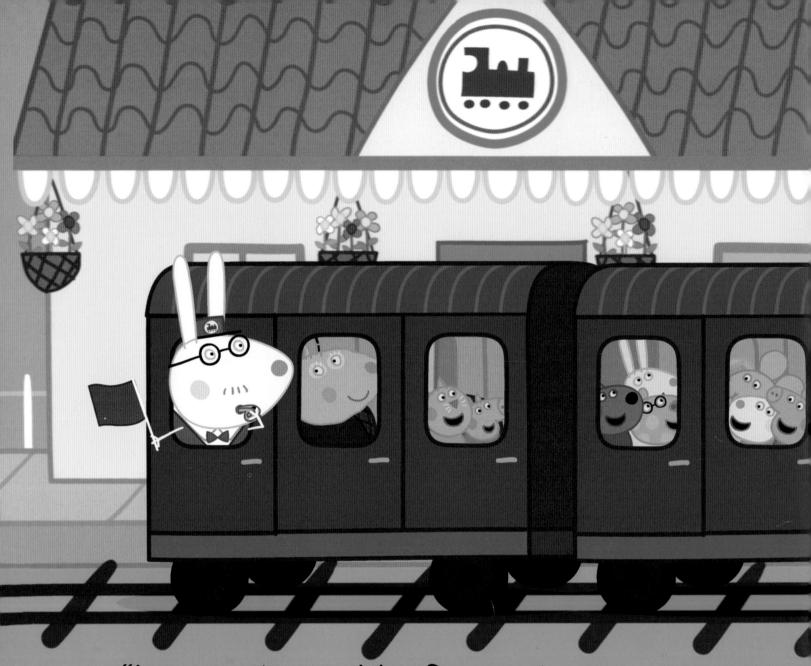

"All aboard!" calls Miss Rabbit, the train driver,
as the train pulls into the station.
The children and Madame Gazelle jump
on to the train and take their seats.

Toot!

The train pulls out of the station and heads down the hill.

Madame Gazelle gives the children an activity sheet. They have to spot a boat, a signal box and a tunnel.

Just then, Peppa says, "I can see Grandad Dog!"
"Ahoy, there!" Grandad Dog calls.

"Hooray!" the children cheer, and then they tick "boat" on their activity sheets.

Pedro doesn't feel very well, so Madame Gazelle lets him go to the front of the train. Miss Rabbit lets him wear her hat and drive the train for a bit, which makes him feel much better!

The train puffs slowly uphill.
The train puffs quickly downhill.
"Wheeeee!" cry the children.

The train stops at the junction to let Mrs Duck
and her friends safely across.
"A signal box! That's on our list!" says Peppa.
"Hooray!" the children cheer, and then they tick
"signal box" on their activity sheets.
The train sets off again. Toot! Toot!

Suddenly, it all goes dark.
"Ooooh! We're in a tunnel," Peppa says.
"A tunnel is the last thing on our list!"
The children tick "tunnel" on their activity
sheets and give a cheer. "Hooray!"

"Last stop!" Miss Rabbit calls.
"But, Madame Gazelle, how will
we get home?" Peppa asks.
"We are home, Peppa!" Madame Gazelle replies.
The train has gone in a big circle, so they are
right back where they started!

"Tickets, please," Mr Rabbit says, one last time.
"Pedro, can I have my hat back,
please?" Miss Rabbit asks.
When Pedro lifts up the hat, there is his ticket!
"Oh, that's where I put it," Pedro says,
and everybody giggles.